BUD'S CHRISTMAS WISH

&

MIRACLE

By

Ashley Nemer

Bud's Christmas Wish
Version 3
Edited by Katia Vodin
Cover Callie Morris
Profile Photo David Garcia
Copyright © 2013
Ashley Nemer
www.ashleynemer.com[1]
All rights reserved.

A product of the Art of Safkhet
www.artofsafkhet.com[2]
Published July 2014

---

1. http://www.ashleynemer.com

2. http://www.artofsafkhet.com

Also by Ashley Nemer

Kemah Sunrise
HoneySuckle Love

Maverick Touch
Maverick Touch The Cat
Maverick Touch The Highway
Maverick Touch The Adventure
Maverick Touch Jail Break

Novella & Short Stories
Bud's Christmas Wish / Miracle
Under The Moonlight
Wolf Pack

The Blood Series
Blood Purple

Blood Yellow
Blood Green
Blood White

The Ones
The Ones Who Lived

Watch for more at https://www.ashleynemer.com.

Table of Contents

Dedication

In life, there are far too few people who know the real meaning of love and who are lucky enough to find that soul mate and discover their life's journey together. I have two sets of grandparents who have done just that. I watched the four of them love, honor and cherish each other through richer or poorer, in sickness and in health. They are the light that everyone searches for when seeking true love. This short story is dedicated to them. May everyone be as lucky as they are and find true happiness with their spouses.

To Joe and Elaine, Pete and Marietta, thank you for the shining example of what love really is.

And for my late Grandpa Pete, I will always remember to "Pray for the Irish."

BUD'S
CHRISTMAS WISH

Part One

Lucy sat in the plane looking out the window at the Atlantic Ocean. She couldn't believe she was actually moving back to Ireland. Every year her grandparents had asked her to visit and she would put it off. Now she would be living there. She didn't have much of a choice since her granddad had fallen ill, but it wasn't like she had anyone back in New Orleans waiting on her. It had been two months since her parents had died, two long, trying, sad and painful months. She remembered the sound of the knock at her door when the officer came to inform her of the accident.

Knock. Knock. Knock. Lucy had awoken up from her sleep and walked over and opened the door. She looked into the eyes of the officer who removed his hat before speaking.

"Ms. O'Toole, may I come in?" His voice had been firm yet soft; she stepped aside as he entered the living room. He had taken a moment before telling her the news.

"Your parents have been involved in an accident along Interstate 10. They were in a taxicab that was involved in a crash with another vehicle. They have both been rushed to the hospital."

Lucy couldn't remember what he said after that, she'd started to zone out as shock sank in. She remembered he'd instructed her to gather her purse and an overnight bag. He escorted her to the hospital where she had been taken to a waiting room. She'd sat there for eternity an as they operated on her parents. Her father's surgeon was the first to come out.

"Ms. O'Toole, I'm so sorry we did everything we could. His lungs collapsed and there was nothing we could do to save him."

She remembered a nurse pulling her into her arms and holding her but recalled nothing the doctor said. She cried on that strangers shoulder as the second doctor walked up to her. This time she was informed her mother's heart gave out in the middle of the operation, when they had to remove a piece of metal that was lodged in her chest.

They were gone, both her beloved parents, dead. Someone called the Chaplin and before she knew what happened she had being whisked away into his office. No words had been exchanged as she held onto his hand and cried. The officer tracked them down inside of the Chaplin's office and began to relay what happened to Lucy.

"The person who hit the taxicab appears to be under the influence of alcohol. He is being arrested and processed as we speak. The assistant district attorney will be in touch with you to go over the trial and what will happen next. Do you have someone who can stay with you, any grandparents or aunts and uncles?"

"No, my grandparents are in Ireland and are ill."

"Any friends?"

"Yeah. I was supposed to pick my parents up from the theater tonight after I got off of work. I forgot and went out with my friend. This is all my fault."

"Lucy, this isn't your fault, you cannot blame yourself." The Chaplin said. The men tried to reassure her that in situations like this she was the victim and not to be blamed. She didn't want to hear about that though. All she saw was the fact her parents were not around.

"I'll take you home Ms. O'Toole and if you need me to notify the officials in Ireland, I will take care of that so your grandparents can be informed."

Yes, Lucy remembered the day like it was yesterday. She elected to have her parents bodies cremated and the urns were wrapped securely in her luggage. This was going to be a long journey. Her granddad had been diagnosed with CHF, whatever that was. All she knew was they needed her and her life in the States had come to an end.

Her plane left New Orleans airport at two forty-one in the afternoon. Of course there were no direct flights so she first had to switch planes in Chicago. The next stop after that was DC and once she landed there she had only an hour to switch to her final plane. That flight left at nine o'clock. Now she was bound for Ireland. She looked at her watch, it was one a.m. She had another eight hours left in the air. Lucy took out her blanket and pillow then propped her head against the window. Closing her eyes she let her mind take her away from thoughts as she fell asleep to the humming of the jets.

"*L*ucy me darling! You're here!" Alastar wrapped his arms around his granddaughter; he loved the sight of her and missed the day she could easily be tossed in the air and placed on his shoulders.

"I assume Bud took care of ye after the plane."

"Yes Granddad, he did. A complete gentleman."

"Aye he is, I have been tellin ya lass there are nothing but fine suitors in Ireland. Now ye will see what I've been saying."

Bud stood back watching the reunion as he brought her luggage in from his vehicle. She was exactly how Alastar had described her. Maybe this arrangement wouldn't be so bad after all.

Part Two

Two Years Later

*T*his time of year was the worst for Lucy, everyone was jolly and celebrating. She never had a desire to participate in this kind of celebration anymore. Not after what happened with her parents. The past two Decembers she had to relive the accident and for once she just wanted to let sleeping dogs lie.

Lucy used to love Kilkenny in the month of December when she was a child. She remembered riding in the sleighs with her granddad while he pulled it behind a cart, going up and down the hills, she would laugh with him all day when they went out on their sleigh rides. Growing up all she ever heard from him when she hadn't visited in a while, "Come back ta Ireland, ye will love it. Tis the best scenery in all of the world and ye true love and soul mate are here, mark me words. Raise a right healthy family ye will." That's what her granddad always told her. He wanted to see her married off more than she wanted to put forth the effort. Men were not worth the hassle, they required too much attention and she wasn't ready for that.

Alas, that's what her granddad 'used' to say. What she wouldn't give to hear those words being hollered through the house one more time.

"Grandmum, are you ready to go? I need to drop you at the McPherson's before work."

"Coming Lucy, hold onto ye britches."

"I just don't want to be late at the tavern; you know the crowds start pouring in this time of year. We could use the extra tips."

Lucy's grandmum, Hannah, was a feisty woman; she was pushing eighty-five and never stopped to let time and old age catch up to her. She managed the local garden at the market and outran most of those young men when it came time to harvest their crop. The only problem with Hannah was she hated to drive. Lucy was stuck taking her everywhere. Not like their town was large by any measure of the land. At most it ran two square miles. On occasion Lucy had to take her into Dublin which was about a ninety minute drive. Again there were worse things in this world and at least Hannah was still here and alive, so she could spend time with her.

"Come on Lucy, stop ya day dreaming, didn't ye say we were late? Chop chop youngin."

"Yes Grandmum, sorry, come on."

Lucy helped Hannah into the car and backed out of their drive. She loved this city, it was much more peaceful than where her parents had raised her. Many stories are told of New Orleans and how wonderful its history was but nothing compared to Ireland.

"What were ye dreaming about lass?"

"Nothing, Grandmum."

"Aye, ya are fibbin, out with it."

"Just granddad and how much I hate this time of year. Nothing new. Promise."

Hannah watched Lucy as her focus stayed on the road. She was proud of her and everything she'd been able to accomplish since coming back to Ireland. Not everyone would give up what they knew to take care of a dying granddad. But that was their Lucy, always there for everyone even if it was at her own expense.

"Okay Grandmum here you go. I'll pick you up tonight after my shift. Don't stay out too long in the cold I don't want you sick."

"Lucy ye forget I've done this me whole life. Don't ya worry."

Hannah kissed Lucy's cheek then left the car and walked up to the McPherson's door. Lucy waited till she saw her slip inside before driving off to the tavern. Lucy worried about her and wondered what she would do if anything happened to her. Hannah was all the family she had left in this world.

"*L*ucy, Lucy, Lucy, lucky loving Lucy."

"Bud, Bud, Bud, big burly Bud." Lucy laughed as her favorite customer walked up and gave her a hug.

"My lass ye are looking wonderful today."

"Thanks Bud, you want your usual?"

Bud looked her over and smiled wide as she led him to his booth.

"If me usual includes a date with ya, then aye!"

"Bud, we have been over this, I don't date the clientele."

"Then I'll stop coming here, I'll hit the pub in the next town over."

"Now we can't have that, you're my best tipper!"

Bud wiggled his eyes at her grinning, "And why do ye think that is Miss Lucy?"

"Oh Bud you're awful; behave and I'll get you your beer."

Bud watched as she went behind the counter and put the drinks on her tray. She moved in a smooth fluid motion, like she was dancing around the floor. She never believed him that he was serious about her but this week he was going to make her see. She was going to be his, one way or another.

"Don't stare too hard, Bud, you will burn a hole in my pants."

"Don't ya tease me lass, I wish."

Lucy sat his beer down and gave one more smile before leaving to help with the other customers. Bud was a good looking man, tanned, tall and with dark hair. All the farmers around here were tanned, all year round. They didn't stop working for the winter season, just found other ways to make a living.

Bud had a reputation of being the town lush. At first she found that hard to believe because he was in charge of the city's tow trucks but Bud did show up in the bar every day. She liked the attention he gave her, who wouldn't? Everyone needed someone to show them a bit of attention and throw compliments their way, even maidens who worked in taverns.

What's wrong with you, just say yes. Lucy thought to herself. Back home she was carefree and fun but, since the accident, she didn't have it in her to be carefree anymore. Sure she wanted to be a normal adult, one with a life and friends, but she couldn't bear the thought of letting another family member down. Her grand mum needed her. Dating and going out with people her own age would take time away from Hannah. She hadn't been able to spend a whole lot of time with her granddad before he passed and she regretted that. She knew her time would come but for now she had to focus her energy on her grand mum.

Looking at her, Bud asked "Lucy, I'd like to take ya out tomorrow night. What do ya say, one chance tis all I'm asking?"

"Bud, why are you so insistent on us going on a date?"

"Aye, it is Christmas time Lucy, let someone take care of ya for once. One night that's all I'm asking. Canna turn a guy down if it's his Christmas wish can ye?"

She let a sigh escape her lips, she didn't want to turn him down, she wanted to have fun but Hannah was home and would be alone.

"You know my grand mum is at home, what would I do with her?"

"Ye can bring her, me cabin's big enough for the lot of us." Bud took her hand in his and stroked her fingers with his thumb. The skin on skin contact from him set her body ablaze with desire. Her lips parted for a smile.

"That be an aye lass?" Bud asked hopeful.

"Fine. Just one night. But we have to come home at the end no staying at your place!"

"Aye, aye, aye, whatever ye say lass!" He leaned in, kissing her cheek. "Ye won't be regretting this. I'll show you and your grand mum a right good time. Picking ya up at seven lass, be ready."

"*Lucy*, why am I going with you? I can stay here and be fine."

"I've already told you I'm not leaving you Grandmum. It will be fine, dinner maybe a movie. You won't be in the way."

"Of course I'll be in the way; the lad wants to see you, not us!"

"Stop that! He knows you are important to me and he's fine with it, I asked, nothing to worry about."

"Lucy I love ye but I am not going on a date with ya clainne. That's final. Now go get ready. Ye need ta look ye best."

Hannah left Lucy's room and went about her business. She couldn't understand what Lucy had been thinking, insisting on a chaperone for the date. She was aware of the times and how customs had changed. She started pulling out pans and baking items to start a loaf of bread. She wanted the house to smell fresh and delightful when Bud came to pick her Lucy up. The quickest way to an Irishman's heart is his stomach. Her mum taught her that and she was planning on proving to Lucy the importance of a strong young chap.

As she finished making the dough she heard a knock at the front door. Looking at the clock Hannah saw it is exactly seven. She liked a man who showed up on time.

"Lucy come downstairs, he is here" She called up the stairs. Turning to the door Hannah opened it to see at the tall man who displayed a welcoming smile to her.

"Mrs. O'Toole, you look wonderful. I hope you are ready for a fun evening."

"Mr. Doran please come inside, Lucy will be down in a wee bit. I regret to inform ye that I am feeling a bit under the weather tonight and am gonna have ta pass on a lovely evening. But you and Lucy should still go and have a wonderful time."

"Am sorry to hear ye are ill Mrs. O'Toole. I don't have to take Lucy out tonight."

"Stop right there, yes ye do. Ye two go along and have a great time, promise me ye will keep her out late."

Bud laughed at what she was saying. What did she think he was taking her to do?

"Aye, will see what I can do ma'am."

"Grandmum I still think this is a bad idea. I don't know what he is expecting from me" Hannah and Bud turn toward the stairs as Lucy walked down talking, oblivious to the fact he was in their foyer.

"Lucy dear, Mr. Doran is here already didn't ye hear me call up to ya dear?"

Lucy stopped mid pace down the steps and she looked over and saw him standing there beaming. "Oh sorry." She tried to play it off with a smile and felt her face flush in embarrassment.

"Not to worry, ye look wonderful and I expect nothing." He couldn't stop smiling at her, the way her face was pink with color was intoxicatingly charming. "Your grandmum said she is feeling under the weather and won't be joining us. I hope you are okay with this."

Lucy shot Hannah a concerned look which quickly turned to annoyance when she realized what was going on. "Are you sure you won't come?"

"Oh no dears, ye go on out the door. I'll just head to bed. G'night ya two."

Hannah shoved them out of the door before Lucy was able to make any objections. On the stoop Lucy turned back looking at the house in a bit of a shock.

"I've not known her to act like this before. I hope she is okay."

"I am sure she is fine. Shall we?" Bud extended his arm up to her as she grabbed it and they walked to his car. "Do ye like ta eat lamb? I have an exquisite rack simmering at me cottage. I hope it suits ye preferences."

"I do like that, I am sure it will be good. I'm sorry that my grandmum backed out. She was not sick a bit ago."

"I think she just wanted ye to spend some time alone with me. She made me promise to keep you out late. Right funny good woman she is."

"Oh God, I'm so embarrassed. I can't believe she said that!" Lucy started to bury her head in her hands while Bud let out a hearty laugh.

"Oh lass don't ya worry she's a wily one. Ye donna be ashamed, ye grand mum loves ya. Come on lets go have dinner."

"*A*ye Mary, he picked her up and left with her. He seems like a nice lad. I hope Lucy gives him a chance."

"Do you think she will ever loosen up to have some fun?"

"Aye she needs to but how can we convince her that the accident isn't her fault?"

"Maybe Bud can help with that, who knows but she's getting ta be too old ta not have a man. Good luck Hannah."

"Thanks Mary, I'll fill ye in tomorrow on how it went."

Hannah hung up with Mary McPherson and went back to the kitchen. She wanted to make sure the bread was finished before she went to sleep. If things went according to plan she would go to bed and wake up to Lucy coming back home smiling and happy. Hannah diligently worked in the kitchen for an hour and once she was pleased with her work she went into the living room and started building the fire. The house was silent, nothing was making noise. In these moments she missed her husband and son the most. It always hit her when she was alone and that's how she preferred it, grieving in peace.

She stacked the logs of wood like Alastar had taught her to do, for the best fires. He wanted to make sure Hannah was able to survive long after he was gone. Alastar and Hannah both had accepted the realization that his heart had weakened and it was only a matter of time until he would be gone. Heart disease was the leading cause of death in Ireland but they never thought one of them would fall victim to it. "Alastar, I hope ye are guiding our Lucy tonight, the lass needs a good lad around."

Hannah lit the starter log and went back to get a cup of hot chocolate. The temperature was just below freezing and she needed the warmth in her bones. She was getting old and really hated coming to that reality. Like everyone she had wanted to stay young forever but then life set in, aches in joints, health issues, a whole laundry list of stuff. She knew the importance of companionship in the later years of life. It was almost as vital as food and shelter.

She walked back into the living room and put in a tape of her son. She refrained from watching old home movies around Lucy but this was her favorite recording of him at Christmas time. Little Jonah just before he turned ten. He had still believed in Santa Clause and the Tooth Fairy. Still thought of his parents as everything he ever needed. Alastar and Hannah missed their son when he took the job in the states working for an entertainment company that produced movies. They never made him feel guilty about only seeing them once maybe twice a year for the last fifteen years, they were proud of what he made of himself.

Hannah didn't cry for her son tonight, no she celebrated his accomplishments and drank to his full life. *She had wanted more children but that unfortunately never happened. They never really knew why, the doctors simple explanation was that things like that just happened. They poured all their love into Jonah and, by the time he was eighteen, he was a man to be proud of. He met Tilly shortly after his nineteenth birthday. He hadn't looked at the girls much in school and claimed he was going into the Church. Then he had one glance at her vibrant red hair and had fallen hard. He was ready to give up his life's dreams and become a husband and a father.*

Hannah and Tilly were cold to one another at first. Hannah had been proud of her son for wanting to follow in her brother's footsteps and join the seminary. Hannah associated his change of heart with the arrival of Tilly so it took a while, a few years actually, for them to first warm up to one another. Hannah and Tilly were polar opposites, where Hannah tended house and took care of everything for her men, Tilly had Jonah help cook and clean. Jonah seemed to like that they were equal but it just felt wrong to Hannah. She eventually saw past the flaws and chose to be happy her son had someone to love. The best thing Tilly had done was provided her with a grandchild. Lucy was the pride and joy of every O'Toole. They doted on her every chance they had till Jonah moved them to the States.

Hannah eventually drifted to sleep on the couch while thinking of these memories. The fire crackling in the background gave her a soothing comfort as she spent her first night alone in over two years.

*B*ud opened the car door for Lucy as they stepped out onto his drive. She looked at his lawn, the brick siding of the cottage and the well-kept concrete of the drive, every nuance was tended too. It was obvious Bud took time and effort in the things that mattered to him. He opened the side door to his cottage and they walked into his kitchen. He had tiles floors, not the tile looking vinyl but real tile blocks. The molding along the floor boards was accented in a light blue while the walls were painted an off-white color. He had dark blue curtains pulled along the windows of the kitchen; they clearly had been washed and pressed recently, the seams of each section were still neatly creased.

Bud watched Lucy look around his home, an appreciative expression on her face. She roamed though the kitchen, he watched her hands dust the counter tops, her gaze traveling the walls.

"Your place is spectacular, simply beautiful. Did you design this yourself or was this set like this when you moved in?" Lucy's asked when she looked up at him and noticed he was smiling at her.

"I built this home with me father. He and I laid every brick, tile and did all the spackle that ye see. T'was our last project we did before he retired. He owned the local construction company before selling out. Me mum, she helped pick the colors. She said a good lass will appreciate all this. I've lived here for just over three years."

Lucy walked to the table and ran her hands along its side; the place settings were out and correctly placed in each of their proper locations. She touched the cotton napkin that felt fresh and clean. She laughed for a moment thinking back to a commercial she used to see in the States that used that slogan, "Fresh and Clean", she loved soap commercials.

"I am glad you approve of me home. Me father always said 'One's home is his castle so maintain it as such.' That's what I've done."

"I do approve, it's wonderful, and what you are cooking smells especially great." She felt like she was in sensory overload. Everything she saw and touched was creating a reaction within her. Her nose was just now catching a whiff of all of the delicious smells that were all through the quaint kitchen.

"It's not quite ready, let's take a tour and when we return I shall give you a feast."

Lucy watched as he extended his hand and took hers in his grasp. He pushed open a swinging door and they walked into the living room. The layout of the room was perfect, not too big but definitely not small. He showed her the hallway where pictures of his family decorated the walls. He had his living room and hallway painted in a light yellow with the windows covered in light green drapes. Everything felt open and spring like. Bud moved them toward the back of the cottage where the two bedrooms were located.

"Do you want to look inside them? I would hate to insult ye and presume ya do."

Lucy laughed and nodded, "Of course, I've come this far, I want to see the rest." She didn't know what to expect the rest of the house was perfectly quaint and charming.

"Aye, once I show ye me bed lass, ya will not want ta leave."

He had a wicked smile on his face that for some reason warmed Lucy to her core. She knew he was teasing but couldn't stop smiling at that comment.

"I think I'll risk it."

Bud opened the door to his room and Lucy mocked her bravery as she crossed the threshold. She saw his elegant oak bed frame and matching dresser and television stand. The fireplace in the corner with fresh flowers on the mantel was a nice touch. "You are right, I don't want to leave. This is the best room in the house."

Bud smiled and walked her over to the chair next to the fireplace and motioned for her to sit. Lucy did as he wished and, when she sat, she sank into the leather. It was as soft as sheepskin.

"I want to thank you, Lucy, for giving me this chance. To show you I'm not like they say I am. That image isn't me. I'm a simple man who has done nothing but craved you from the first moment I saw you at the airport."

"Bud."

He held his hand up to silence her.

"No Lucy let me finish. For what, almost two years now, ye have been serving me my drinks. Every night I come in there. Do ye think I am really the town lush? I have two drinks at most and

I never have women. I come there to see you and to interact with you. I would listen to ya granddad talk about stories of ya when he was healthier and he told me you were just the lass for me. And he was right! He never let me go a day without telling me about his wee lass."

She sat in the chair watching him. The sincerity in his voice, the words he said, and the look in his eyes when he spoke about her granddad made her stop and think, did he really only have two drinks a night? How had she not noticed this before?

"Please Lucy, give me a chance, one night ta show ye that I can fulfill ya dreams and give ye everything that ya could imagine ya needed. Everything ye could ever want."

"I said yes, I came here tonight."

"Aye ya did Lass, but ya were to have ya grandmum with you, I hadn't planned a night of wooing with ya grand mum here. I'll need one more night."

"She's not here now though, you can have your night."

"Ever so stubborn aren't ya lass. Just like ye granddad."

"I did learn from the best," she beamed at him. He loved how she looked when she smiled. He would watch her at the bar when talking with others. The way the lights shimmered in her hair, her teeth pearly white, smiling for everyone. She was everything a man thought of when he pictured the perfect maiden. Except for that stubbornness, that was all her granddad.

Lucy stood up and grabbed onto his hand and pulled him towards her. "I can smell the food, let's go eat and maybe I'll let you woo me tonight."

Bud reached around her and placed his hand at the small of her back and then leaned over and put his arm behind her legs and lifted her up in the air. She laughed and kicked her feet a bit in protest.

"The food can wait. You cannot. I can't let ye leave till ya know how much I care."

*A*s they lay there, Bud holding Lucy's body tight to his own, she felt his whiskers run across her skin as his chin moved up and down along her neck. She had never felt that before, not with anyone. Bud was exceptional in more ways than one. There was something about him that made her tingle, aside from his whiskers. There was something magical about this time spent with him. She couldn't explain it but she could feel it.

Her thought turned to her mother who had always told her that a woman's first time should only be with a man who was deserving of her.

"Are ye still awake?" Bud asked softly as his hand ran down her leg, tickling her skin.

"Yes I am." She felt him running his whiskers down her back and then kissing her skin, again those whiskers, she could get used to that feeling.

"Lass, ye should be asleep with me. What's keeping ya up?"

"Nothing I was just thinking about tonight. You made my first time special; My mom always said it was supposed to be special."

"Lass, how many times must I tell ya, I care about ye and will keep showing ya I do."

Lucy smiled and pulled the covers up toward to her chin, she let her body settle against his as he put her hand with his, intertwining their fingers.

"Goodnight Lass."

"Goodnight Bud."

And with that Lucy let herself fall asleep.

Part Three

"*W*ake up sweet lass, time for a surprise." Bud said while kissing Lucy's ear. He heard her murmur something incoherent, as he tried stirring her again. "Lucy, wake up, we need to get going so we aren't late."

Lucy turned her head to the side and cracked her eyes open, the clock indicating it was 4:15 in the morning; she'd only been asleep a few hours. "Bud, it's early, come back to bed." She pulled the covers over her head trying to tune him out. What was he thinking waking her up before the crack of dawn?

"I said up!" Bud smacked her on her butt playfully, right before he removed the covers from her body. "We donna want to be late. C'mon."

Lucy grumbled under her breath but got out of bed and dressed; slipping her shoes on and pulling her shirt over her head she went to meet him in the kitchen. She watched as he put a basket together full of different kinds of food. She could smell the strawberries and instantly perked up at the smell of hot chocolate.

"What are we doing Bud, a picnic?"

"You'll see lass, just put ya coat on, we donna want ya to get sick do we?"

Lucy went to hold the door open for him when he went to pack his car with the basket but he swatted her hand away.

"Aye, lass, stop that. Let me handle the door. You just go warm ye self in the car."

"Always the gentleman Bud." She said smiling at him. She went and sat in the car, it was already running and warm. She saw a camera in the console and two scarves on the dashboard."

Where is he taking me? She thought to herself.

"Alright, all packed we are, let's go!" Bud said as he sat in his driver's seat and smiled at Lucy.

"And where is it we are going? It's not even sunrise yet."

"Precisely sweet lass, precisely. We are going to watch the sun come up like God intended it to be seen."

"What's that mean?" Lucy said with a nervous laugh.

Bud grinned at her, "Why sweet Lucy, do ya no' trust me? I would never do something ta hurt you."

"It's not that it's just...I've learned when men get *that* look in their eyes, no good comes of it." She said in a playful tone.

"No good eh? That is exactly what I planned."

He backed out and drove for about an hour out into the country side. Lucy continued to smell the fruit and her stomach grumbled, reminding her that they had forgotten to eat dinner last night. She was about to ask if she could get a bite when she saw what they were approaching. Standing tall and beautiful was a hot air balloon.

"Oh my" she said, her breath wispy and shocked.

"Hope ye aren't scared of heights."

Bud parked and grabbed the scarves, camera, and basket as Lucy got out of the car. They walked up to the balloon and an older gentleman smiled toward them and opened the basket door. Bud guided Lucy inside and she sat on the bench that was against the far wall. She watched as Bud paid the older man and watched as he walked away.

"Are you ready to watch the sunrise? It will be up in about half an hour."

"Yeah, I am. Can you, fly this thing?" She looked around the basket very cautiously.

"Aye, my family used to take us flying constantly as children. You're in good hands." He smiled at her then gave the signal. The old man began releasing the ropes as Bud started the hot air balloon's ascension into the sky.

"Open the basket lass; there is a thermos of hot chocolate and two mugs. It's going ta get chilly the higher we go."

"And strawberries I see."

"Aye, and some grapes, nothing heavy just a bit of things to snack on."

She poured the hot chocolate out and carefully stood, Bud laughed at her light heartedly watching her take nervous steps toward him. "Why Lucy, this basket is solid you donna have to move carefully lass. Ya are safe."

"I've just never been in one before, I don't know these things."

He chuckled to himself again as he took a drink out of his mug. There was a little light off of the horizon starting to break the blackness. He pulled Lucy over to him, wrapped his arm around her and pointed with his finger out to the horizon.

"There she comes lass, are ya watchin?"

"Bud I've never seen the sun like this."

They watched as the rays soared across the black canvas, the perfect mixture of red and yellow molding into the orange horizon that developed. Bud leaned his head down and kissed her neck, her soft skin tantalizing his senses. His lips brushed up to her ear where he nibbled lightly. He kissed along her jaw and finally turned her around. She faced him and, as the top quarter of the sun encroached on the sky, he leaned down and kissed her. His tongue breaking through her lips and tangling with hers. She wrapped her free hand around his neck and he held onto her tight as the sun rose in their background.

"Thank you for finally saying yes lass."

"Anytime Bud, this was wonderful."

They watched the sun rise and, as the bottom of it broke free of the ground, he began their descent back. Lucy felt a bit of her heart warm as this man kept overwhelming her. She was unsure of herself sometimes but this seemed like it could be real. The old man was at the landing site when they touched down. Bud threw out the rope as the man secured the balloon. They walked to the car and Lucy looked back over her shoulder taking one last look at the trip of a lifetime.

He pulled into her driveway and reluctantly let go of her hand to shut the engine off and put the car into park. His left hand lingered on the gear shift wanting to touch her again. The smooth silky feel of her skin drove him wild. He wouldn't forget how she felt under him last night, how their bodies moved together in a synchronized pattern. It was as if they were meant to be together mixing their two bodies as one.

"Thank you for everything, it wasn't um..... what I was expecting.... but it was really breathtaking." Lucy said with a sweet smile on her face and a lot of hesitation in her voice. He liked seeing her stumbling for words. He knew he caught her off guard and that was how he wanted to keep her.

"Would you like to come in for breakfast? I mean, I know how this looks but grandmum won't care."

"I would love ta come in. Thank ya lass." Bud opened his door and quickly raced around to the left side of the car and opened Lucy's door. "Careful, its slick, the snow's turned ta ice overnight."

Lucy took the hand that he offered and smiled up to him as she stepped out of his car. She hadn't felt this carefree and happy in a long time and, as they approached the house, her face started to flush thinking of running into her grandmum.

As if her grandmum knew her thoughts, the front door opened and there she was smiling back at them.

"Well good morrow ta ya. Had fun I take it?" Hannah was never one to hold back, she always said what she was thinking even if it embarrassed Lucy.

"Grandmum!"

"What? I told him ta keep ya out. Come in, ye both will catch ill." Hannah opened the door and motioned them inside. She was grinning from ear to ear knowing that this was the best sign she could have that Lucy finally cut loose and had fun.

"Bud may I get you a coffee?"

"Actually Mrs. O'Toole, Lucy promised me breakfast, didn't ye." He smiled over at Lucy whose cheeks blushed at the mention of breakfast.

"Yes, I did." Lucy said with a soft laugh.

"Now now, ya two just sit down and get warm. I have ye breakfast already prepared."

"How did you know we would be back now?"

"A grandmum knows these things lass. Sit, warm ye self. I'll be back." Hannah rushed out of the room, her skirt flowing in the air as she moved faster than Lucy could remember her moving in months.

"Is ya grandmum always this excited about breakfast?" Bud asked while reaching over and taking Lucy's hand in his.

"No, I think she is this excited over the fact I brought a man home."

"Progressive grandmum she is."

"She's just simply afraid she will die and I'll not have anyone around to take care of me."

"She doesn't need to worry about that." Bud said with a soft and serious tone.

"That's what I've told her but she wants me to find a man. I tell her I don't need one."

"Would it be so bad if ya had one around?"

She looked at him and thought for a moment before speaking. "It isn't that it would be 'bad' it is simply not what I am putting my energy towards right now. My concern for the time being has to be her. She needs someone to help care for her."

"She looks like she is doing fine as it is. Ya deserve a bit of fun and excitement don't ya?"

Lucy smiled up at him, his words made her stomach tingle setting off her anxiousness. She knew what he was meaning but wasn't ready to address that just yet. Thankfully her grandmum came back in the room and signaled for them to join her in the kitchen.

The three of them sat quietly and ate, the food was delicious and Bud knew this was where he was supposed to be. "Mrs. O'Toole, will ye excuse me, I need ta get back home. There is something I forgot."

Lucy looked at him with a puzzled expression, what did he forget? She had all her items with her.

"Of course dear. Lucy, please see him out."

The two of them left the table and walked to the front door. Standing in the foyer Lucy looked up to him with a questioning tone, "What's going on?"

"Ahh, don't ye worry lass, I'll be back. But there is something I promised I would do for ya granddad one day and I've just remembered I needed to do it."

Bud rushed out of the home and into his car where he drove off to his cottage. He remembered the day he made the promise to Lucy's granddad about marriage but he never thought she would give him a chance. It's now or never to him. This was the moment. Alastar knew one would present itself and Bud just needed some faith.

He made it to the cottage and walked into his bedroom and opened the safe he kept in his closet. Pulling out a soft black velvet bag he loosened the string and then poured the contents of the bag into his palm, his grand mum's engagement ring. The center stone a full 1 ct. and the six surrounding stones .5 ct. each. The diamonds were set on a gold band with a pattern of vines etched into the gold. Bud returned the ring to the bag and left his cottage on his way back to Lucy's.

He had been hesitant before last night's date but now he knew this was right. His parents and grandparent's relationships were predetermined and in the end they had more love than anyone else he'd seen. He knew this would work, and more importantly, he wanted this. Inside the car he drove and recited a little speech. His father had told him from a young age, "The O'Toole girl will be yours, our families made a pact long ago." Then when she returned to take care of her granddad he came home one day beaming with excitement. "Did ya go see her? Back from the states and more lovely than could be. Ya will win her over and make her yours."

He saw their cottage grow bigger as he drove closer. His heart was beating fast. He needed to maintain his courage to carry this out. Up the driveway and into park went his car. He marched up the front steps and before he could knock on the door Lucy opened it up for him. He walked inside and looked to Hannah with a smile. She gave him a nod, her blessing, and he turned to Lucy.

"Come sit down Lucy." He motioned her to the stairs and waited until she was sitting.

"I don't understand what all of this is about. What's going on Bud?"

"When we were just babes our granddads made a pact, our families were to be united. At the time, the only way to do that was through marriage and since ya father and mine couldn't marry for the obvious reasons, they promised ye and me to each other. Before ye granddad died he made me swear that I would fulfill the promise. I didn't know if I wanted too, I'd heard of ya my whole life but didn't know how ye would act or be like once we met. That's why I kept coming to the tavern."

"Are you trying to tell me.."

"Wait Lucy let me finish."

Lucy bit back her thoughts; she wanted to let him talk but also wanted to scream. She looked at her grandmum who was smiling from the other side of the foyer. It was obvious she had known this whole time what he had been doing. "I wasn't mad at him for making me promise after I met ya. Your voice, your skin and your smile, are everything that would make any man feel lucky. I most likely would have done this sooner but ya never would go out with me. I didn't want to ask and tell ya about all of this till we had a proper date."

Lucy couldn't believe what she was hearing; would her granddad really bind her to someone, a stranger? Well he wasn't a stranger anymore especially after last night. She felt her face blush at the thought of things they did while together.

Bud reached into his pocket and pulled out the black velvet bag, he opened it and pulled the ring from inside. Lucy's heart stopped for a second when she saw how beautiful it was.

"Lucy, I know this is quick, unexpected and insane but sometimes ya have ta take a chance on love, on what our parents and grandparents felt when their fates were decided for them. So on this Christmas Eve's day, would ya do me the honor of agreein' to be my wife?"

Hannah smiled as she watched the two interact; she had been worried that this might never come to pass. She had known Bud's family all of her life and knew this was meant to be. She took her hand and placed it over her heart and gave a loving smile and nod to Lucy. Lucy looked into her grand mum's eyes and could tell this had been what it was about this whole time.

"Bud are you sure?"

"Aye Lucy, as sure as I'll ever be about anything."

Lucy looked to her grandmum for guidance one more time; all she saw was her encouraging smile and pure excitement and joy on her face.

"Yes Bud, but on one condition..."

"Anything lass, name it."

"You must promise to love me and care for me all my life, just like my granddad did for my grandmum."

Bud let out a bellow of a laugh as he slipped the ring onto her finger. Picking her up and kissing her deeply he simply said, "I do."

BUD'S
CHRISTMAS
MIRACLE

BUD'S CHRISTMAS MIRACLE
Version 3
Edited by Katia Vodin
Cover Callie Morris
Copyright © 2013
Ashley Nemer
www.ashleynemer.com

A product of the Art of Safkhet
www.artofsafkhet.com
Published July 2014

Part One

There were birds signing outside and children laughing in the streets. Spring was starting, and nothing would stop the magic of Ireland when it came to Bud and Lucy's wedding. She would never forget how her granddad, Alastar, had orchestrated this whole thing before he died. There had to be magic here, otherwise they never would have found each other.

The aisles were laced, the flowers were displayed, and the parish was ready. The church bells rang loudly, alerting the town to the ceremony. Many parishioners piled into the tiny chapel to witness their union.

"Grandmum, is my veil on right? Is it straight?" Lucy looked herself over in the mirror nearly one hundred times before she felt she looked perfect.

"Aye, lass, come on. You're beautiful. Now let's get ye married off." Hannah pulled on Lucy's arm, lined them up at the edge of the hallway, and signaled to the organist to begin the music. Lucy's heart was racing as she opened her eyes and saw Bud standing there.

The two women walked in unison down the aisle. Lucy looked around at all the familiar faces that had been a part of her life for two years now. Her heart was heavy with grief, with her parents and granddad missing, but the woman who held her up walking down the aisle beside her was all she needed.

"Who presents this woman for marriage?" The priest asked.

Lucy felt the warm touch of her grandmum just before she responded, "I give Lucy away."

Most of the ceremony went by in a daze; Lucy couldn't take her eyes off of Bud. Dressed in a perfectly pressed suit, black jacket, baby blue shirt, and pinstripe pants, he made the most handsome groom she had ever seen. As gorgeous as he was, the one thing that stood out was his smile. It melted her heart to see him looking back at her. She loved that he had loved her even before she'd known he was interested, all because of her granddad and his dying wish for his clainne.

The minister jarred Lucy's attention when he told them to stand and face each other.

"Do you Bud Doran, take Lucy O'Toole to have and hold, for better or worse, in sickness and in health, until death do you part?" the minister asked.

Bud looked at Lucy, his heart beating fast, overwhelmed with happiness. His body warmed with the smile she gave him when she looked up into his eyes. "I do." It was the easiest thing he'd ever said.

The minister turned to Lucy and began repeating the same words. Bud's attention never left Lucy's perfect face as her words, "I do," rang through his ears. The sounds of the parishioners in the church murmuring and rejoicing at their declarations filled both Lucy and Bud's hearts.

"I now pronounce you man and wife. Bud, you may kiss your bride!" The priest proclaimed.

Bud took a step toward Lucy. He wrapped his arm around her waist and pulled her close to him. Leaning his head down he took her lips softly and gently with his own. He heard her gasp for a moment, and then felt her hands wrap around his neck. His other hand went around her back, and he picked her up, placing one hand under her legs. Holding her dress in place, he carried her down the aisle.

"You can put me down, Bud. I can walk, you know," Lucy teased at him. She felt her heart fluttering with excitement as he held her close at the altar inside the church.

"No lass, I donna think I can." Bud kissed her again, this time longer, more passionately. "Ya see, now ye are mine and I'm never letting ya go."

He shot that grin she'd come to adore and laughed. "Well, you have to let me down for a minute; we have a party to attend." Lucy ran her hand down his cheek and then cupped his chin. She loved him, and she knew this was all because of her granddad.

"Ya grandmum and my mum can handle the guests. We donna need to be there." Bud carried her down the aisle and over into the corner and tried to steal a few silent and private moments but was quickly interrupted when the guests started walking out of the main area of the church.

"Bud, Lucy! Come over here!" Hannah called out to them.

Lucy let out a disappointed groan, and they both turned their heads and saw her waving her hands in the air, trying to draw their attention. She was standing with Bud's mother and father. Everyone's focus was on them.

"See, my husband? I told you, party first, alone time later."

Bud let Lucy slip from his arms to go be with their family. He already felt empty with her out of arm's reach. He was doomed, and he knew it. With a proud stride he sauntered over to the women and smiled at his mother and Lucy's grandmum.

"Well shall we go dance?" Bud asked the ladies.

Hannah and Lucy were quick to say yes. Bud's mother was more nervous. She was not as outgoing as the O'Tools.

"Come on, Mum, I'll spin ya and make ye forget ya nerves." Bud grabbed his mother's hand in one palm and his wife's in the other and then escorted his women into the adjoining parlor for some drinking, dancing and dinning.

*A*fter a few hours of socializing, Lucy was feeling worn out and exhausted. She had kicked her shoes off and tossed them into one of the corners of the room, forgetting where. She looked over her shoulder and saw her grandmum looking out of the window, gazing at something. Lucy got up out of her seat and made her way over and sat down beside Hannah.

"Penny for your thoughts?" She let her hand rest on her grandmum's and realized she was looking at the hills and a few ducks playing on the green grass.

"Ahh, me clainne, it's nothing." Hannah patted Lucy's hand and smiled at her.

"Don't tell me it's nothing. I see you looking out there." Lucy watched a few ducklings playing together and smiled. It was a perfect sight on her wedding day.

"Aye," Hannah sighed out, "married ye granddad out on that hill. Just missin' him is all." Hannah squeezed Lucy's hand again and stood up. "Come, let's find ye husband and send ya on ye way."

"I'm not ready for the night to end just yet." Lucy looked out at everyone smiling and laughing together. It was all about to change. The reality of marriage and life would begin as soon as they walked through those doors and out into the great unknown ahead of them.

"Lucy, 'tis time. Bud's waitin'. Now let's go and make ya granddad proud."

"I never would have thought three years ago back in New Orleans that I would be here today, happier than I could imagine." Lucy gazed out onto the hill and suddenly felt a twinge inside her heart.

"What's wrong, Lucy?" Hannah asked.

"Suddenly I miss Mom, Dad and Granddad."

"They are all looking down on ya and smilin'. Now come on."

Hannah pulled Lucy out onto the center floor in front of everyone. They were met in the middle of the floor by Bud, his outstretched arm patiently awaiting Lucy's.

"Ye ready to start our adventure together, lass?" He smiled down at her, his eyes twinkling in the light.

"Always with you, Bud, always."

Lucy stepped in close and let her body press up against Bud's. The band started to play a slow beat, and within seconds she and Bud were moving in rhythm to the music. She felt light as a feather in his arms; nothing was going to get into their way.

When the music died, Bud leaned in, kissing her on the side of her head, against her hair, whispering, "Alright, lass, tell everyone goodbye. We have plans to keep."

Lucy and Bud started to walk towards the doors leading out of the parlor. Everyone had begun lining up, ready to send them on their way.

Bud's mother came up to Lucy, gave her a hug, and kissed her cheek, then did the same for her son. Lucy couldn't help but notice that her new mother-in-law was crying. She hoped they were happy tears. Her mother-in-law stepped aside, and the couple began walking down the procession.

Rose petals flew through the air, landing on Bud and Lucy's heads and shoulders. When they got to the end, Lucy looked into her grandmum's eyes. She could see tears of joy on her cheek.

Hannah nodded at the two and opened the door to the vehicle for them. She watched while Bud whisked her clainne off into the sunset.

"Alastar, you did it again," Hannah whispered to herself as she waved them off.

Part Two – Nine Months Later

"*B*ud, you missed the turn!" Lucy held onto the handle of the car, bracing herself while Bud quickly spun the car around.

Hannah's light body slid across the backseat, and she laughed at her clainne. Ever since she had become pregnant, her sensitivities had increased. "Lucy, ye need ta be more calm. That yelling isn't good for ya wee one."

"Grandmum, the baby can't hear me, and he missed the turn! We are going to miss our ferry!" Lucy was all worked up. Her cheeks were flushed and her pregnancy glow made her face shimmer in the light of the sun.

"Lucy, donna get worked up. If we do, then we will catch the next one, or go on the morrow. Stop fussing." Bud he reached over and rubbed his hand on her stomach in an attempt to calm her. His smile was big and bright. He knew it always soothed any worries Lucy had.

"Oh, don't you use your Irish powers on me, Mr. Doran. I know what you are doing. Now just get us to that castle. I want to see the place of my granddad's family's roots."

"Ya granddad would turn over in his grave if he knew you proved his family was from England, Lucy." Hannah was laughing from the backseat. She was picking up the fruit that had rolled out of the picnic basket on that last turn; Bud really was making a mess of things in the backseat.

"Aren't we all a little English, Grandmum? I mean, we all speak the language, and wasn't all of this the same country at one time or another?"

"Bite your tongue, Mrs. Doran! No child of mine will be told he is a native Englishman!" Bud gave her a pointed look; he starred straight into her eyes for a solid five seconds before bursting into laughter and leaning over, kissing her head. "Alastar would really get a kick out of this, wouldn't he?"

"He would." Lucy smiled up at Bud. She picked his hand up off of her stomach and placed a kiss on his palm. "And besides, you don't know that we are having a boy. It could be a little girl."

"Nonsense, Dorans have men. Why, look at me. I'm an old chap!" Bud pushed his chest out smiling big, trying to distract Lucy from her looking at the time.

"Are you trying to tell us that the Dorans have no bloodline girls in the family? I find that impossible." Lucy poked at his side playfully.

Hannah shook her head in the back seat. "Oh, your poor mum, what you must have been like as a child. I feel sorry for ye, lass, if ya babe is anything like his father."

Lucy and Bud both laughed, and Lucy gave out a sigh of relief when she saw the sign for the exit to their ferry.

"See there, Lucy, I told ye I'd get us there on time. Ye of such little faith," Bud teased at her.

"Aye still think doing this trip while you are two weeks from delivering was risky, Lucy," Hannah said from the backseat.

"Grandmum, the doctor said I was okay to take a drive. It isn't like I'm flying to the States!"

"She wanted one last trip before the wee one was born, Hannah. Canna talk her outta it." Bud flashed a smile over to Lucy, who smirked at him.

"You two stop worrying. I'll be fine."

They pulled onto the Hollyhead, UK ferry and paid the toll. After the car was secured to the boat, the three got out and walked to the sky deck of the ship.

"Lovely Lucy, do ya need anything ta drink, maybe a hot co-co ta keep warm?" Bud pulled her close to his body and held her against him. It was chilly outside. There were flurries starting to fall in the air, and some were landing on their skin.

"No, Bud, I'm fine. Come on, let's sit down. It's a long trip. We don't want to stand the whole time."

Bud sat next to her and watched while Hannah sat in the chair across from them, next to an older man. "I think your grandmum has found her entertainment for this two hour ferry ride," Bud whispered into Lucy's ear while pointing over at the elderly man Hannah was speaking with.

Giggling, Lucy pulled on Bud's hand and brought it into her lap. "Bud, stop pointing. No one likes to be singled out! But it's nice seeing her smile like that. I even think she might be flirting a bit."

"Aye, it is. Maybe we can sneak off and I can make ye smile like that too, lass." Bud wiggled his brows at her and grinned.

"Stop. You're incorrigible." Lucy was smiling at him. Her cheeks were wide, and her heart was fluttering. She loved when he acted like this, carefree and fun, like he was a teenage boy in love for the first time.

Bud pretended to tip a hat he wasn't wearing. "Thank ye, lass. I doth love ta make ye smile." He moved his hand up her stomach and paused when he felt the tiny pressure against his hand. "Lucy, lass, my boy's kickin'!"

Lucy watched the gleam in his eye; her heart warmed knowing he was this excited for their child. "Yeah, the baby has been very active for the last few days. And you don't know it's a boy. Not yet."

"He feels strong, like his father." Bud palmed her stomach and rubbed the spot where the little kicks had come from.

"My wee one needs a name, lass."

"Not until we know the gender, Bud. We have been over this. Patience, my love. Now let's enjoy the view on the water and maybe take a nap; you know how tired I've been getting lately."

Bud tucked her in close to his body and held her there. This must have been what Alastar meant when he'd told Bud of the arraigned marriage and promise of happiness, how life would be one day once they found each other.

The two hours passed, and Bud watched Hannah mingle with the older gentleman. It looked like she was having fun and enjoying herself with another man for the first time in years. The wind was blowing steadily, and the temperature had taken a drastic drop. The attendants had released the stairwell to allow the passengers access to go back down to their vehicles. He could see England up ahead in the distance.

"Lass, we're here. Wake up, lass." Bud nudged at her with his free arm. She had been sleeping for an hour, and his right arm had fallen numb underneath her.

"Mhmm are we there yet?" she murmured with a sleepy sigh.

"Aye, come on, lass. Let's go ta the car and warm ya up." He helped her stand, and they walked a few steps where they were met by Hannah who was beaming while talking to the same gentleman that had kept her company throughout the ferry ride.

"Grandmum, who is your friend?" Lucy jabbed Bud with her elbow, trying to get him to stop snickering over her shoulder, and grinned at Hannah.

"This is Cristian." Hannah looked from him to Lucy and then continued with the introductions. "Lucy, my clainne, and her husband, Bud. Can you believe what a small world this is, but he is on his way to Stafford as well. That's where he's from." Hannah attempted to keep her tone calm, but Lucy could detect the hint of excitement in her voice with each word that she spoke.

"My, it is a small world. We are going down to the car. Are you ready to go, Grandmum?" Lucy and Bud started to make their way toward the door and noticed that Hannah wasn't moving with them. "Grandmum?"

"You kids go ahead; Cristian has offered to keep me company the rest of the way to the castle." Hannah had her arm wrapped around his and the same smile still beaming across her lips.

"Come on, lass. She'll be fine," Bud said in a low whisper to Lucy.

"But, Bud…" Lucy hesitated, looking from her grandmum to Bud then to Cristian.

"Go on, kids. I'll meet you there. The four of us can have that picnic in a couple hours."

Bud and Lucy watched Cristian escort Hannah across the floor to the other door leading to the stowed cars and then down the steps.

"Do you think she will be okay, Bud? I don't feel right." Lucy's stomach felt tied in knots watching her grandmum walking with the stranger out of the room.

"Aye, lass, I do. Cristian is a good solid name. 'Sides, we'll find which car he's in and follow 'em. Make sure they go the right way." His hand moved to Lucy's lower back. He guided her out of the room and down the stairs to their car. There was an oomph when the ferry docked with the land.

"I don't see them, Bud!" Lucy's panic had set in. Her eyes were scouring the cars, looking for Hannah. "Wait, there, right there." She pointed over to the blue car in the back corner on the far row. "Do you see them?"

"Aye, lass, I have 'em. Donna worry. Just relax; that worry isn't good for the baby." Bud shifted the car into gear and started to move forward. He let the other cars pass him until he was behind Cristian's car. "See, lass, there we go. Now rest ye eyes, and I'll wake ya when we've arrived at Stafford."

Lucy reached back into the backseat, pulled a blanket from the bag on the floor, and wrapped it around herself. "I'll try, but I doubt I'll be able to rest much."

Bud turned the CD player on and let the soothing music start to play, the classical songs drifting through the speakers. He smiled when Lucy's hand came out from the blanket and reached for his. He let his thumb run over her fingers as he held onto her. They drove in silence, and after fifteen minutes he looked over and saw her eyes were shut and she was back to sleeping.

*T*he change in the road woke Lucy up. Her eyes caught sight of the castle up ahead and the nervousness she had felt before was gone when she saw the same blue car in front of them.

"It's much bigger than I thought it would be." She smiled over at Bud and then focused her attention back on the castle.

"Look at it; this is where my ancestors are from, Bud. Isn't it amazing?" Admiration poured out of her when she spoke while looking around her ancestors' castle. She wrapped her arms around her stomach while the baby's kicks were increasing. Her heart was warming her body, thinking about how much her granddad would secretly enjoy this trip if he was there with them.

Bud pulled the car up beside the one Hannah had been traveling in and shut the engine off. He stepped out of the car, walked around to the left side, and opened Lucy's door. "Come on, lass; let's go on the walking tour. They have those things ye can listen ta and follow along with."

"I want to get the picnic from the backseat first, Bud. That way we don't have to keep coming back and forth."

"Ahh fine, lass, let me help ya." Bud collected all the fruit that had rolled around on the seat, put it inside of the basket, then pulled the sack of blankets out, and with both things in hand he turned and looked at his bride. "Aye, lass, now can we go?"

"Yes, Bud, now we can go." Lucy put her arm around Bud's, and they walked over to where Hannah and Cristian were standing.

"We've been waiting for ya two. Ready ta go in?" Hannah said to them.

Lucy noticed that her grandmum had her hand wrapped around Cristian's, and it looked like Hannah was glowing herself. *Had Grandmum been lonely this whole time?*

"Well, we're all here now, so we can start. I wonder where in this castle the Lord of Stafford stayed." Lucy's eyes were surveying the brick wall they were standing next to. "Can you believe this is over a thousand years old? It looks so good!"

"I'm sure they have someone tending to it, lass." Bud guided her over to the line where they picked up the walking tour headphones.

"Well of course they do, Bud, but look at it, so tall, so big. It's amazing."

Bud enjoyed watching her light up with excitement as they walked into the castle and put on their headphones.

"Might I suggest we start over here?" Cristian said to them. "This is one of the best starting spots of the tour."

"Ye have been on it before?" Hannah asked him.

"Aye, several times, m'lady, several times."

Cristian put his hand under her elbow and escorted Hannah ahead of Bud and Lucy. They watched him help Hannah with her headphones, and they slowly started walking ahead of them.

"Lass, ya grandmum looks happy."

"I know, Bud; isn't it great? Come on." She tugged on his hand. "Let's not miss out on our tour."

They spent the next hour walking along the corridors of the castle. Lucy looked inside every open area she could, delighting in all of the history she could manage to soak in. The baby kicked the entire way, and her body and mind felt over stimulated with the excitement. They found the room used for the kitchen, and she tried to picture life without electricity.

The lights that were installed in the castle started to flicker after they arrived. There was a whistling sound that started to emerge from the outside, and Lucy was curious to find out what it was. They walked over to a window and saw that the parking lot was covered in snow.

"Oh, Bud, look at the snow! Doesn't that make you want to rush outside and play?"

"Nah, 'tis makin' me think of our fireplace with you by my side in bed."

Lucy blushed at his comment and then felt another kick in her stomach. "This one sure is active today. She or he hasn't had this much movement in such a short time span before."

Bud grinned ear to ear and simply said, "'Tis cause my boy is ready to come out and play."

"Oh, he better not be; we still have two weeks!"

"Doncha know, lass, us Doran men do what we want, when we want."

"Oh, I know, but this one is a girl. She will take after the O'Tools, prim and proper."

"Lucy, how'd ya like this bedchamber for home?" Bud teased at her. He pointed to the bed that was made out of wood and animal bones mixed together.

"Oh, I think not, Mr. Doran. Ya got another thing coming if you think that's going in our home." She laughed. "What were they thinking, using bones on the bed? That's just so wrong."

They bantered the entire way and couldn't get enough of it. Towards the end of the tour, Bud reached out and took her hand, holding her back from the rest of the people.

"What's wrong, Bud?"

"Mhm, Lucky Lucy, come with me." He pulled lightly on her hand and slipped inside one of the rooms that was roped off from the tour.

"Bud, we're not supposed to be here!" she proclaimed.

"What's a little fun on vacation, lass?" He pulled her into his arms and ran his hands down her back, cupping her bottom and leaning in, kissing her sweetly.

She got lost in the kiss for a few minutes before she heard noises outside of the room. "Bud! Someone will come in."

"Shh, lass." He kept kissing her, cupping her face, and stroking her cheeks with his thumb. His free hand moved down to the side of her round stomach that was bulging out. He softly stroked her while he laid kisses along her jaw. "Aye, lass, I love you."

"I love you too, Bud."

He pulled away from her, looked down into her eyes, and smiled. "Shall we go find ye grandmum?"

Lucy simply nodded, and they started to walk with the rest of the tour group towards the exit when Lucy felt a pulling on her stomach followed by a wave of pain pulling in her uterus. She felt her body tightening and the urge to let out a cry start.

"Bud."

He stopped and turned around. His face went white when he saw his bride in distress. "Lucy, what's wrong?"

Her mouth gaped open for a few moments before she started mumbling, "The baby, Bud, the baby!"

With a frantic worry, Bud started looking around the area in search of a chair for her to sit in. He tried to remain calm as he grabbed one of the stools from outside and brought it back to her. "Lucy, sit down, rest. You don't need to worry. I'll go get help."

"Hurry, Bud, she's coming!"

Lucy watched him run off into the outside crowd, and she tried to focus on her breathing. She went through the calming strategies they had taught her in the birthing class. She found a focal point inside the hallway and locked her stare on it.

Her breathing started to quicken and she began the breathing exercise. Lucy tried to regulate her contractions and efforts to slow the process down. It felt like it was going faster than expected. She heard a commotion outside, growing louder, and then she saw her grandmum walking through the door with Bud in tow.

"Grandmum! Help!"

They both raced over to her and each took a hand. "Shhh, Lucy, we got ya."

"Help's on the way, Lucy. Don't push!" Bud told her. "They're stuck in the snow storm that just hit. Just wait a bit more, lass."

Lucy looked up at him with a pleading stare, "Can't we drive to them, or the hospital?"

Bud shook his head slowly back and forth, "No lass, sorry, love."

"I," Lucy breathed in and let it out, "can't wait. Coming, now."

Hannah looked around and saw a circle of people starting to form around them. She pointed to the corner behind the crowd near the exit. "Tha corner over there. More privacy."

"Nay, there's a room over there." Bud pointed to the room that he and Lucy were just in.

"Ahhhh, noo!" Lucy squeezed their hands tightly and started to push. It was a natural response, and she couldn't stop it.

"Now, she's coming now. Help me undress."

Bud helped her onto the flood and slid her pants down while covering her as best he could with them once they were off. "Lass, I dunno what ta do."

Hanna came over and pushed him aside. She forced him to move up to Lucy's head where she could rest her head against him instead of the floor.

"Oy, Lucy, I see the head. 'Tis time, one big push on three."

Bud took Lucy's hands and let her squeeze them. She was propped up on him as he supported her.

"Grandmum, I'm scared."

"None of that, now push, lass, push! One, two three!"

She strained at first. The initial push felt like her skin and insides were breaking apart. She thought she was tearing her body apart. At the second push she started to feel some relief from the constant pressure, but it wasn't until she gave the third push that she found her pressure subsiding.

Lucy let out a cry, and shortly afterwards the baby emerged. The cries that the infant made started to echo in the castle.

"Oh my, Lucy, it's a boy!"

"Aye! 'Tis what I've been sayin'!" Bud kissed her head and peered over her shoulder to get a glimpse of his son.

"Is he okay, Grandmum? Can I see him?" Lucy wiped the tears away and then felt a sudden rush of happiness flush through her.

"Bud, that's our son."

"Aye, lass, that's our son."

Part Three

"*E*ldon Peter Doran, that's his name," Lucy said, peering into his crib.

"'Tis a fine name, lass. Alastar would have loved it. So would your mum and da." Hannah rubbed Lucy's arm and smiled down at her great-grandson.

"I can't believe we were stuck in the castle for twelve hours. At least the hospital only made me keep him there two days so we can all spend Christmas Eve together."

"Aye, 'tis good."

Eldon started to whimper and the two women both reached out for him. Hannah smiled and then pulled her arms back so Lucy could tend to her son.

"Shhh, there, there, Pete. You're okay. Momma's got you."

"Pete?" Hannah asked.

"Yeah, Eldon's his formal name, but I'm gonna call him Pete. Do you like it?"

Lucy watched Hannah nod her head and smile.

"Ah me clainne aye do. Welcome home, Pete. You're already so loved."

"Mind if we join?" Hannah and Lucy turned around to see Bud and Cristian standing in the doorway, watching them.

"Sure," Hannah exclaimed. She reached her hand out for Cristian and pulled him close to her side. "Have ye seen my new sonny-boy today?"

"Aye, we took him down to the tavern for a beer earlier," Cristian teased.

"Hey now, there will be none of that for a good ten years, you guys." Lucy rocked a now sleeping Eldon back and forth in her arms and went to sit in the rocking chair. She suddenly felt her granddad's presence and knew this is what he had wanted for her all along. She looked down at the sleeping babe and silently thought, *Eldon, you and your granddad now have something in common; you're both English.*

"Hey, Bud?"

"Aye, lass?"

"Merry Christmas."

There was that smile that she loved coming from him again. "Aye, Merry Christmas."

THE
END

Don't miss out!

Visit the website below and you can sign up to receive emails whenever Ashley Nemer publishes a new book. There's no charge and no obligation.

https://books2read.com/r/B-A-NDUF-OTMS

BOOKS 2 READ

Connecting independent readers to independent writers.

Did you love *Bud's Christmas Wish / Miracle*? Then you should read *Under The Moonlight*[1] by Ashley Nemer!

Zara's fate had been decided thousands of years before her birth. She is now fighting against time and family to reclaim the decisions that will ultimately shape her destiny.Sentenced to live an existence in the Underworld, mated to a man she despises, Zara must find a way to overcome the Gods and their curses, with love as her only guide.Can James, a handsome and rugged sailor, help Zara break the bonds of magical spells or will she end up mated to Xander, the Son of Satan?Take a dive Under the Moonlight to see where love can take you

---

1. https://books2read.com/u/bxqo2q

2. https://books2read.com/u/bxqo2q

Read more at https://www.ashleynemer.com.

Also by Ashley Nemer

Kemah Sunrise
HoneySuckle Love

Maverick Touch
Maverick Touch The Cat
Maverick Touch The Highway
Maverick Touch The Adventure
Maverick Touch Jail Break

Novella & Short Stories
Bud's Christmas Wish / Miracle
Under The Moonlight
Wolf Pack

The Blood Series
Blood Purple

Blood Yellow
Blood Green
Blood White

The Ones
The Ones Who Lived

Watch for more at https://www.ashleynemer.com.

About the Author

Ashley is married and lives in Houston with her husband and their two children. She and her husband have been together for over a decade and he brings her more joy than she could ever imagine as a child. Their two children have filled their lives with laughter and excitement on a daily basis. She loves to read and has been hooked on the romance genre ever since her life long best friend Laura gave her "Ashes to Ashes' by Tami Hoag to read when they were in high school. Ashley finds her strength through her family, especially her parents. They always support her in life, they push her to strive for greatness. There once was a motto that Ashley heard in her youth through her Taekwondo life 'Reach for the Stars' and that is what Ashley has always done. It was through her upbringing that the values Ashley has and display's came from. With her Parents always cheering her on in life she was able to grow up having faith in herself and her ability to conquer the world.

Author Links

http://www.ashleynemer.com

http://www.facebook.com/ashleynemerauthor

http://www.facebook.com/ashers83 (Add Friend)

http://ashleynemer.blogspot.com

https://twitter.com/ashleynemer

https://www.goodreads.com/user/show/2897381-ashley-nemer

Read more at https://www.ashleynemer.com.

About the Publisher

SAFKHET READERS

Safkhet's Pride - Our Street Team (Open to twenty (20) members)

Here, readers will interact with the authors and have behind the scene chats to get the word out there about our book releases. We will have contests and special swag that is offered ONLY to our Street Team.

Requirements:

At least once a month post about one of the books released from The Art of Safkhet.

At least once a month share one status by an author.

When a new release comes out, recommend it to at least five friends on Goodreads.

What's in it for you:

All new releases the month they come out will be sold at a discount price. E-books will be 50% off and print books will be 30% off.

When SWAG arrives all members will get first grabs at the items

Special contests for print books or gift cards held just for members of the Street Team.

Safkhet's Elite - Our Beta Readers (Open to fifty (50) readers only)

Here, readers will get advanced readers copy (in e-book format)

Readers will tell us which genre's they want to read and we will email them their ARC.

Genres are:

Paranormal

Contemporary Romance

Erotica

Science Fiction

Mystery

Mythology

Poetry

Requirements:

Upon receiving an advanced copy of our new release, you will need to post your honest review with in fifteen days of its release and place a link to that review on the appropriate authors Facebook page.

If you cannot read the ARC in a timely fashion please email Grace (info@artofsafkhet.com) so she can make note. Missing more than two e-book distributions in a row without reason will have you removed from Safkhet's Elite.

Your review must be honest. We are not looking for all 5-Star reviews but honest opinions and thoughts about our work.

By joining this program you agree to not share, distribute or sell the Advanced Readers Copy of our work.

Some of you will want to be both, a Pride member and an Elite member. At this time we are asking that you pick one or the other. This may change in the future but for right now we ask that you just pick one. If you are interested in either of these please let us know.

You can join Safkhet's Pride by going to this link https://www.facebook.com/groups/222253454608269/. This will take you to our Facebook group where we will post the different information.

You can apply for Safkhet's Elite by commenting on this post with your name, email address and genre's you want to read and stating which of Ashley, Stacy, Anabella, or Niki books you liked most or by sending Grace an email at info@artofsafkhet.com with all of the information.

Thank you for taking the time out to inquire about our new Readers Groups and we hope to see 70 new people in the near future!

* 9 7 8 1 3 9 3 1 7 0 3 1 0 *